Many thanks to Matthew Small, Dan Saberi, Matt Wingett and Susan Power, and to the usual suspects – Simon Field, Mishkin Fitzgerald, Jeff Prattey, Dara Fitzgerald, Jason Achilles and James Bulbeck for helping Helene through her sorrow and suffering.

Wednesday's Child

Written by Hana Piranha. Illustrated by Daisy Hull.

Chapter One

nce upon a time, in a land called Circan, there lived a royal family; a great dynasty who had grown in power and wealth over centuries.

Even in less fortunate times it can easily be imagined that these rulers had wanted for nothing. The king had more wealth than he could have thrown away in ten lifetimes and the castle he lived in was a monument of opulence. Every item within it was of the finest craftsmanship - the marble pillars that lined the main hall were intricately carved and the floor was studded with jewels. The delicately embroidered beds each held seven mattresses. Chandeliers with hundreds of candles hung in every room, making the entire castle shine brilliantly. The queen, with her dark hair and large, striking blue eyes, was said to be the most beautiful woman in all the land. Shortly after they wed, she was delighted to give birth to a baby girl who they named Helene.

The royal line of blood had bred beauty, grace, and strength. However, cruelty and blind ambition were also inherent traits of people who sought to hold such supremacy. It must be known that however dazzling the surface of their lives might be, many of the family, including the king himself, had done ugly things – things that were cause for bitter hatred. But now times were good and the king and queen rejoiced in their fortune.

Shortly after the birth of Helene, the queen began to have a strange dream that recurred every night. Waking up with a start to a burning smell, she saw flames closing in around her bed. She jumped up and snatched her daughter from the crib, running through what seemed like endless corridors. Fire bounced from mirrors and flames licked at hanging paintings, reflecting diabolically in the eyes of the subjects. As she ran out with the child in her arms, she looked down and, in horror, the face she saw was not a face, but a raw lump of flesh with two hungry eyes staring straight into hers, blood collecting at the tear ducts. The mouth began to open but there were no teeth, just a blackness that seemed to lead nowhere. From it came a monstrous hiss:

"Pearl to pebble, silk to hay
Night winds bear your joy away"

As these words sounded, she was sucked into the hole of the mouth and found herself again in her own bed. But the echo of the voice still pulsed around her ears and her body went cold with terror as she felt something stroke her cheek. *I'm dreaming*, she thought, but though she willed herself to open her eyes, she lay there petrified as the stroking continued. Then she felt a soft breath on her face, and able to bear it no longer, screamed.

Awake at last, the queen sat up in bed, heart racing, and covered her mouth with her hands. She picked her child up from the crib and rocked her gently.

"No-one's going to harm you, as long as I'm here," she murmured.

But every night that the dream repeated itself, these words were said with less and less conviction.

 few weeks later, a celebration took place in the event of Helene's christening. The doors of the palace were opened, welcoming people from far and wide. Fashionable members of the court floated around like exotic butterflies, ready to gossip, and laugh, and flirt with old world noblemen, heroes of the great wars, merchants and explorers, bringing gifts from dark and magical lands. Violins played and the hall was filled with music and laughter. The wine flowed freely, and for a while the queen forgot her misgivings. However, among these guests was a simply-dressed old woman who attracted little attention. No-one noticed as she approached the child's crib. She caressed Helene's cheek with a bony finger and breathed in the princess' ear:

"Pearl to pebble, silk to hay
Night winds bear your joy away"

Though barely a whisper, these words floated, as if on a cold breeze, to where the queen was standing ten feet away. She felt the blood drain from her whole body but before she could rush to her daughter's side, she collapsed in a faint.

A multitude of feverishly fluttering fans greeted her as she regained consciousness but she knew she couldn't share the cause of her distress. And sure enough, back at the crib there was nothing to be seen but a few cherry blossoms scattered around the sleeping child's head.

Chapter Two

elene grew up with all the refinements befitting a princess. She was beautiful, with a slender frame and large, dark eyes, curtained by eyelashes so thick that you could almost hear them flutter off her cheek when she blinked. She was quiet and graceful and carried herself with the assurance of one who had never been denied anything. Above all, she was an accomplished musician who played the harp and sang charmingly. However despite all of this, there was a void in the princess' life. While it was no surprise that the king was indifferent to a daughter, it was strange that the queen never saw the princess, leaving her education and wellbeing entirely up to nurses and governesses. At the rare times that Helene would have an audience with her parents, her mother looked at her with an overpowering sadness. Helene grew up with a feeling of mystery surrounding her. She learned to stay silent and ask no questions. But in the reliance on her inner world, the princess developed a formidable strength and resourcefulness that no-one else could see.

Two days before Helene's eighteenth birthday, the queen summoned her daughter to her chambers for a rare interview.

"My darling," she said, though her face flinched slightly at this endearment, so unnatural on her lips. "I hoped I would never have to say to you what I am about to say. But in the years since your birth, I have looked into the effects of... childhood curses."

The last words came out hesitantly, in a low tone, and the queen wouldn't meet her daughter's eyes. The feeling of trepidation that this inspired in the princess was accompanied by a rush of anger that her good breeding instantly suppressed.

"Dearest Mother," she said, and these words felt equally strained. "I hope that you might tell me plainly what you have discovered."

The queen sighed.

"I believe that something evil visited you as a child. I pray with all my heart that I am wrong. However, if, against hope, I am correct, this curse will take effect as you turn eighteen. Tomorrow at the stroke of midnight, moonlight as you know it will be stolen from you. Your days will be as before, but at night you will be transformed."

Helene searched within herself at these cryptic words and was surprised to find no fear, only resolve.

"Transformed into what?"

"A messenger of eternal sleep, and blood will be your craft."

The queen's voice was reduced to a whisper and Helene could hear the fear in it. She felt a chill begin to rise in her.

"What shall I do?" she asked.

Her mother's eyes, which had been open to the whites, gradually settled, and her rapid breathing regained its control. She led the conversation swiftly to more comfortable territory.

"I have been saving these gifts for your eighteenth birthday," she said. "Firstly, a more pleasant item, customary on the eve of your first ball."

She held out a beautiful locket, which opened to a miniature of Helene's portrait.

"When you meet your true love at the ball, you will give him this gift to remember you by."

Next, she walked over to a concealed object and pulled off the velvet drape to reveal an ornately framed mirror.

"This is no ordinary mirror," she said. "Look into it every morning and it will help you approach every new day with fresh courage. However you must promise to always keep it covered after nightfall."

"One more thing," the queen continued, unveiling a black maple harp with strings of gold. "This too is for you, for when you are married. Use it to serenade your husband every night and it will send him into a deep slumber. Under no circumstance must he discover your secret."

At this abrupt juncture, the queen stopped talking and Helene knew that the interview was over. She had many more questions but the years of silence that had encouraged no outward curiosity constricted her throat. Her mother offered nothing more.

"Well, my love" - these words felt so alien that Helene could almost have cried. "Bad things sometimes happen to good people and we can only do our best with what we have been given."

Following this pointless conclusion, Helene walked back to her bedroom, more lonely than she had ever felt in her life.

Chapter Three

The following night - the eve of Helene's eighteenth birthday - a great ball took place at the palace and kings and queens came from far and wide to honour this powerful family. The hall was full of splendour and joy. Sparkling candlelight bounced from crystal and glass and Helene glided down the spiral staircase, glistening in the reflection of five hundred eyes. Her white gown enveloped her slender figure and her long dark hair fell heavily down her back. Her eyes shone like dark moons from her face. Everything about her was soft and serene.

In the land of Circan, fate worked in a particular way. As surely as she was to turn eighteen, so it was that Helene was destined to find true love at the ball. And this happened from the moment she locked eyes with Soal, a handsome prince from a distant kingdom. He was exquisite, with a chiselled, pouting jaw and eyes that always looked like they were smiling.

Helene wasn't sure she had seen Soal before, but it was like she had always known he was there and the dances came and went while, in the hidden chambers of her mind, she waited patiently for the moment that he would reveal himself to her.

Then he finally stepped out from the shadow of one of the marble pillars and without a word, took her gloved hand and bent his lips to it. The touch moved like lightning up her arm, across her chest and straight into the deepest cavity of her heart. And from that exact moment, she knew she had finally come of age and that her life as she knew it was about to change. As his eyes looked up, the rest of the world faded. Nothing was real except for the knowledge that he was looking at her and she at him.

"Will you dance with me?" he asked simply.

She nodded and his hand touched her back, and with it came a feeling that she had never been truly whole until this moment. The room blurred around her and all she was aware of was the light touch on her waist and his breath against her cheek. The feeling of aloneness that had accompanied Helene's entire life was suddenly gone.

"I want to share everything with him," she thought to herself. "I know that the more he understands me, the more he will love me." Her mind went into a daydream. But suddenly it was broken by the remembrance of her mother's words. *Under no circumstance must he discover your secret.* And a dark shadow passed over her face.

Soal was equally enchanted by the beautiful dark-eyed princess and had a sharpened awareness of every touch between them. Even of the darkness that crossed her. Then the cloud moved on and the prince and princess delighted in the joy that they had been blessed with.

Courtship moved quickly in Circan and before the night was over, the young couple were engaged to be wed.

Chapter Four

ut before Helene could be swept away by her happiness, she caught sight of her mother from the other side of the room. From within a sea of smiles, the queen's face emerged, pensive, brooding, and staring straight at her. Helene turned to the great clock above the staircase. The hand was already nearing the stroke of twelve. Feeling a mixture of longing and regret, the princess turned to gaze at her love's face for the last time.

Helene unclasped the locket from around her neck and pressed it into the prince's hand. As she did so, he grabbed her wrist forcefully, causing her breath to catch in her throat. His eyes bored into her with such intensity that she felt everyone in the room must notice it; the gaze drove thoughts into her that caused her to blush in such a public setting. Her eyes widened and she opened her mouth to say - what? To implore him to slow her thundering heartbeat? Then, just as abruptly, he let go; and without a word, she drew away and moved gracefully up the stairs. As soon as she was out of sight, the princess took off her shoes and began to run.

No sooner did Helene close the bedroom door behind her then changes started to happen to her body. Her shoulders heaved of their own accord and she doubled over in pain, bones clicking as she felt the skin around them stretching and cracking. To her horror, her shoulder blades began to lengthen and then grow multiple strips of their own, before shredding themselves into smaller pieces, until she realised that she was looking at feathers belonging to a large pair of white wings protruding from her back. Her agony, and the fear of what she had become, increased as she realised that her wings had grown from *inside* her skin, which was now stretched so thinly that it was almost transparent. She tried to touch it but a sudden sharpness caused her to scratch herself. Her hands were changing; becoming thinner; and her dainty white nails were forced roughly from her fingers as sharp black talons grew in their place. She went to drag this new weight painfully over to the mirror but then remembered her mother's advice. The princess sat back on the bed and began to weep. But as she looked down, she saw with revulsion that it was not tears but blood that was dripping from her eyes onto her hands. As she had been reborn through love, so too was she born again through blood and bone, pure with the rising sun and wicked in the light of the moon.

o began the first of many long and lonely nights. Each morning she uncovered the mirror again to see her sweet and pretty reflection. But even as she gazed at the warm sunlight caressing her skin, the horror and shame of what she had become lingered on.

Chapter Five

fter just seven long days of revering the locket Helene had given him, Soal was finally reunited with his princess at the altar. But something in her face had changed. Helene didn't look like a child anymore. From the moment her veil was lifted, the prince was aware of prominent details, features that had always been there but had somehow blended differently up until now. Her eyes, which had always been large and dark, had a hooded effect and seemed sunken into her face. In fact her whole face seemed like it was drawing into itself – it was like her cheekbones were stopping the skin from collapsing.

Love was true - an unchanging emotion in these lands - but against his will, caprice crept into Soal's heart at the sight of the princess, and the happiness that should have accompanied the union of this young couple escaped him. His eyes still smiled but there was nothing behind the smile.

In Circan, renouncing a vow was as inconceivable as being pulled by gravity to the sky. So the appropriate words were uttered and Soal kissed Helene's lips, though he felt an involuntary shudder as he did so - a shudder that was not unnoticed by the princess.

It moved like lightning through her lips, across her chest and straight into the deepest cavity of her heart. And from that single moment, she knew instinctively that the next chapter of her life was to be as lonely as the last.

Soal escorted the princess back to his palace but a cold discomfort had nested itself in the prince's heart and he found reasons to shun his wife's bed. At first he told her that he was tired or unwell but as days wore on and the prince's thin lies became more and more transparent, he knew the right thing to do was to look her in the eyes and tell her directly how he felt.

The princess knew that her demonic transformation was not coincidental with her husband's obvious change of feeling towards her. Tortured by the contrast to her dreams of an intimate bond, the princess resolved to go against her mother's advice.
"I will not live my life as she did," said Helene angrily to herself. "I will not shroud the lives of those around me in uncertainty and obscurity. I love Soal with all my heart and for that reason I will do what my mother could not. I will look him in the eyes and tell him the truth and if he hates me for it, well, at least I will have done the right thing."

But, walking in the rose garden as she turned over this resolution, Helene bumped right into Soal. The prince looked shaken out of deep thought also. This encounter - physically the closest they had been since their wedding day - startled them both. Helene, thrilled by the close contact, looked at her husband searchingly and hopefully. But any pity Soal had felt in his heart was overcome by revulsion at the simple touch of her hand and his desire to tell her how he felt vanished completely. Helene knew this and it hurt her. Exposing the horrors of her curse to the prince was more than she could bear.

oal began to avoid Helene altogether. Shunning her chambers was no longer enough for him and he began to make extended trips away from the palace. The small enchanted harp sat gathering dust, and the beautiful princess had the appearance and presence of a forgotten doll. Helene rarely left her chambers and the courtiers and servants alike wondered at their new, unseen, princess. Inquisitive ears listened to her melancholy songs and the cries of pain that were heard from her room at night. And as the mystery that surrounded the princess grew, so did the whispers throughout the palace.

Days turned into months, and months became years until all the pain and isolation that had at first been so acute slowly numbed into a dull routine. The princess played her mournful songs from morning until night, only stopping just before twilight to take a walk among the blossoming cherry trees that grew in the orchard. Away from the clusters of the blossoming trees, there stood alone a tall tree clad in black bark and empty of even a single blossom.

There was a singular dark beauty to the tree that set it apart from the others, as if it suffered a similar plight to her own. Helene felt a strange connection to it and every evening she would stop and sit beneath it for a while. The thin branches rattled in the breeze, and if she closed her eyes, the princess could almost imagine that it was speaking to her.

One evening as she was sitting under the tree, a great sadness overcame her and she cried out,

"Oh sister tree, sometimes I feel like you are the only one consoling me in my misery."

All of a sudden a gust of wind blew overhead and the gentle rattle of the twigs increased into a scraping of branches. And to the princess' great shock, she was able to discern words.

"Gentle princess, what troubles you so?"

Helene opened her eyes and jumped to her feet in fright. Walking around the tree, she peered closely up into its stark branches, which were now shaking vigorously. "What magic is this? Who speaks to me?"

Specks of dirt were now blowing into her face as the wind around her continued to increase. She closed her eyes again and the strange soothing voice with its gravel tone was as clear as if it had arrived in her mind; as if the wind pushed the words straight into her head.

"My dear, don't be afraid. Tell me, what is it that you desire?"

There was nothing pleasant in this sound and any sense of affinity and calm she had felt beneath the tree had long vanished. *Leave now*, she told herself. But a darker hunger surfaced in her; a recklessness. And so she responded.

"My husband doesn't love me and I suffer in his absence. My greatest wish is for him to want me."

The wind was getting stronger, blustering now, causing the top of the trunk to creak back and forth. Every noise that came from the tree blended into one single tone and the words thundered into the princess' head.

"Well. Maybe we can come to some arrangement."

Helene was no fool. She had a strong feeling that whatever magic it was that caused the tree to speak had been leading up to the proposal it was about to make. Every instinct in her body told her to walk away. But her husband had brought an unfamiliar feeling of powerlessness into her life; a powerlessness that, more than anything else in the world, she longed to conquer. So now that a solution presented itself, Helene didn't stop to think about what it might cost.

"What arrangement do you speak of?"

"Well," the branches shook abrasively, "as you can see, I am barren, but when I feast I produce the most splendid blossoms."

"Feast?" repeated Helene, and the shiver that went through her body was not simply the chill of the wind.

"Although my fruit may be sour, the cherry wine it yields can be very… persuasive…"

The wind was now blowing a gale and thick grey clouds hooded the sky above. The princess gazed up in fear. But still she stayed.

"What has that to do with me?" she enquired, shuddering with a premonition of the next words.

The branches of the tree were now grinding together wildly and the scraping sound they made set the princess' teeth on edge. The words were painful to hear, but still she listened.

"Only with the bleeding heart of a man beneath my roots will I flourish. Bring this to me and in return, the wine I give you will grant your wishes."

Helene struggled to stand straight, so forceful was the wind around her. Thick drops of rain were splashing onto her face like heavy tears and she felt that she had entered a place in her soul that she was not supposed to visit. Her face darkened.

"Oh, wicked tree," she exclaimed. "I will entertain your sinful words no longer."

The force of the wind was now pushing her over, almost pinning her against the trunk, but with an effort she broke away and step-by-step propelled herself back towards the more inviting blossoms of the orchard. As she did so, the wind slowed and the evening sun again touched her face.

But a seed had been planted.

Helene carried on her days just as before, but something was different. The tree's words bounced like an echo around her thoughts.

"You will not beat me," she said to the bloodthirsty creature inside herself. "I will master this curse, though it might drive me mad to do so."

Every night she sat at the window ledge and looked out at the night sky beyond. How good it would feel to stretch her wings, to swoop down against the breeze, to…

"No," she said firmly, gritting her teeth. "I must not think those thoughts."

So she stayed, gazing - hunched like a gargoyle - at the stars. But every night she felt more intensely the weight of the huge wings she was trapped under.

Chapter Six

The princess now avoided the cherry orchard altogether and took a route closer to the servants' quarters. One evening as she was out walking, she heard her name spoken. Quickly she concealed herself behind an apple tree.

"Rumour has it," came a voice, "that the marriage was never consummated."

A dry laugh responded. "Well we know that for sure. But is that really a reason to send her away?"

"My brother has it on good authority," continued the first. "Apparently the prince has paid a visit to his father for consent on the annulment. It's been five years after all. His Lordship is clearly not happy."

These words hit Helene in the pit of her stomach and it took all her effort to stifle a dry sob. Reeling, she walked back to her rooms, the tree's diabolical proposal resounding loudly.

I t was a stormy night and Helene sat at her usual perch on the windowsill, gazing out at the black sky that hung over the castle like a veil of mourning. Gusts of wind howled through the trees of the many woods and gardens that comprised the palace grounds, and in amongst the blustering of leaves the princess fancied she could hear the singular scraping of branches coming from the cherry orchard. Her arms and legs ached with the weight of the warped bones on her body but it was nothing compared to the strain of the hopelessness that she felt in her heart.

"I've got nothing left," she cried, knowing it was weakness that uttered these words. But her will was gone, leaving only the overpowering urge for an escape from her painful nights and empty days. It was at this moment that Helene finally gave in to the dark temptation of her curse. She placed her night-time talons clumsily onto the ledge.

"This is the moment I will determine if I am no longer good for anything" she thought to herself, and she jumped.

How sweet it would have been to fall all the way down and become nothing, but Helene's wings opened and she soared. The feeling of power in the strong winds that surrounded her was a reawakening for the princess, and all the evil feelings she had hitherto repressed rushed into the forefront of her mind and she embraced them.

"This is who I am," she thought, "and I feel good."

She flew over the castle walls, and in no time she was hovering above the forest that had always seemed so far from her window. Her eyes, so sharp in the darkness, focused to seek out any solitary moving objects. It wasn't long before she saw someone wandering through the forest back towards the village, and she dived towards him. When her victim looked up in his last living moments, he thought an angel had come down upon him, so beautiful did she look with her pale eyes and white wings.

He wasn't alive for long enough to see the wings turn red with his blood as she dug out his heart in one elegant movement.

And so the deed was done, and she rejoiced in it. The weight of the corpse was nothing as she flew up and up, back into the storm, freed in this new animal feeling of power and purpose. Her wings were fast and soon she was back at the orchard. With a single scrape of her talons, she buried the heart beneath the roots of the cherry tree. Then she flew deep into the woods where no-one would venture, and discarded the body.

Chapter Seven

unrise finally came and Helene trembled at what she had done.

"I have sold my soul," she whispered to herself.

For three days, overcome with horror and disgust, she stayed in bed. Her mother's mirror remained covered. Whenever she closed her eyes, all she could see was her victim's face and the blood on her wings. So she lay listlessly, haunted by the waves of revulsion that continued to surface within her. But every night she again soared from the window. As the moonlight had been unbearable, now it was the dawn that announced the wretched half of her life. Soon however, unable to bear the sickness of her self-loathing, the princess began to embrace what she had become. Every night she killed and every night she buried another heart under the now-blossoming tree. And every day Helene's dark mood began to lighten with the sunrise until one morning she uncovered the mirror and glared imperiously into it.

"You are not a monster, but a huntress," she said to the raised chin of her reflection.

Finally, Soal returned to the castle. It had been months since Helene had last seen him. Every time he had come back, he was more distant, and this time he wouldn't even look her in the eye. The princess remembered the conversation in the apple orchard and knew she had to act fast.

"This is the part where I reap what I have sown," she said to herself, and she ordered the servants to make wine from the tree's cherries. She had this brought up to her chambers and drank it discreetly.

That night, Soal heard a knock at his bedroom door and to his great surprise, the princess entered. He opened his mouth, about to turn her away, but as he looked upon her face he was stirred with a feverish desire. She beckoned him to follow her to her chamber, and, impatiently, he obeyed. So began their reconciliation as man and wife. Soal forgot his intention to send the princess away. Instead, she consumed his every thought, and every night he visited her bed, where she managed to both satisfy and feed his obsession. Afterwards, the enchanted harp lulled him into a sleep so deep that he never witnessed her nightly transformation.

Each morning at sunrise, Helene uncovered the mirror and gazed into it, but the sunlight on her face no longer shone sweetly. Day by day, she saw herself start to change. Her already drawn face looked sallower, as though the skin was slowly being stretched over her sharp cheekbones. Her eyes gradually appeared more and more hooded. While she still retained her quiet and gentle manner, the expression of innocence in her face was markedly fading. And although she wished to embrace the changes inside herself, she didn't like what she saw.

The gradual shift of Helene's appearance was not unnoticed by Soal. But contrary to her own aversion to her reflection, Soal found her more and more alluring. The sharper her cheeks and the more shadowed her eyes, the more he wanted her. Quite apart from the cherry wine, there was something about her fall from virtue that enthralled him.

However, despite his fixation, the prince started to feel inexplicably unclean in his very soul, and just as he had first resented his wife for his inability to love her, he now started to resent her for the impure feelings she inspired in him.
As time wore on and his craving for her showed no signs of weakening, he began to suspect her of witchcraft. He subtly turned away any food and drink that she had touched, but to no effect. Still his distrust grew.

One day during his ride into one of the nearby towns, the prince passed a placard sporting a crude drawing of a winged creature, with the offer of a reward for information on an "Angel of Death". Upon further enquiry, he was told that there had been a number of disappearances recently. It was probably old women's gossip, they said, but there had been more than one report of something strange flying around these parts after nightfall. The prince had a sinking feeling in his heart and he felt that this was somehow linked to Helene.

During the day he watched her with a closer eye, with plans to continue until she slept. However he realised he was mysteriously falling asleep night after night. Finally one evening as Helene was taking out the harp, the prince secretly placed soft wax inside his ears and pretended to be sleeping. And so, out of one slitted eye, he finally witnessed Helene's transformation into a beautiful and terrifying creature, which was without a doubt the infamous Angel of Death.

oal lay in the bed in horror. Not even an hour ago her touch had given him an insatiable pleasure. He played it over in his head - consuming her gaze, kissing her skin - but now her form was jagged and skeletal and her beautiful dark eyes were a milky blue like nothing he had ever seen before. Beneath his numb disbelief, a dirty feeling surfaced. Above all, he realised the grave mistake he had made in visiting the princess' bed.

"The Jezebel has tricked me," he thought, furiously berating himself. "I knew there was something wrong with her from the start. Oh, why was I seduced by her witchcraft? I should have sent her away while I had the chance. And now it is too late."

As the days passed, Soal continued to sleep with his wife. He told himself he did so as to not arouse her suspicion. But he knew the real motive deep in his heart: he still desired her, though it would have made him sick to admit it. He knew something had to be done. He could no longer send her away. He thought about unveiling her terrible secret and putting her to death, but how could one overcome the shame of having such a wife? So he resolved to kill her himself, secretly.

"I am no murderer," he told himself, with a feeling of righteousness. "She is a demon and must be slayed."

Each night he lined her glass with a different poison but he was unsurprised and almost relieved when none had any effect. Still each night he would come to her chambers, and each night he would witness her transformation. Yet he continued to want her.

"She's a monster and a witch," he said to himself, until it became a kind of mantra.

Each night Helene returned with blood on her wings and the prince was driven almost to madness wondering where she had been.

Finally one day as he was walking down a corridor, he overheard two servants speaking.

"I wonder that she can drink something so sour."

"Well, who are we to question it? She insists on that particular tree. Apparently no other cherries will do."

Soal felt like a fool. It had simply not occurred to him that this wine could be the cause of her spell over him. That night he hid in the cherry orchard and waited in trepidation for the princess to appear. It was late and he was fighting sleep when he felt a rush of air almost sweep him off his feet as a shadow passed over him. And there she was; silent, deadly, and magnificent. Soal watched in horror as she removed, in a single elegant movement, a still-beating heart from her claw and placed it under the tree. Maybe he was imagining it, but he was sure he saw a tremor run through the tree as the blood touched its roots.

The next day, Soal gave orders for the tree to be cut down. Helene's wine was served as usual but the instant the glass touched her lips, she knew something was wrong. In alarm, she rushed down the many flights of stairs, pushing with all her weight through the heavy bronze doors. But when she reached the cherry orchard, all that remained in the tree's place was a burned stump. The tears flowed down her face as she reached it, for although the sinister magic of the tree had drawn out the darkest side of her soul, nevertheless it was the only thing that was *hers*. It knew what she was and didn't despise her for it. The princess flung herself down beside the barren roots, at the place where she had sat so many times before, but now there was nothing to shade her from the accusing sun. She wept because she knew without a doubt what this meant: Soal had discovered her secret and he hated her.

Chapter Eight

uring his trips into the nearby town, Soal heard talk about an old woman in the forest who had mystical powers. Previously he would have scoffed at the idea of devoting any importance to some solitary old hag. But that was before he had discovered Helene's secret, and it's curious how a little trouble can quickly cause a person to value what they formerly derided. So the prince set off into the dark forest to pay the witch a visit.

It was a long journey and the forest was as dark as night. The denser the trees became, the more Soal had a feeling of strange eyes watching him. By the time he reached the hut where the woman lived, his nerves were thoroughly shaken and it took all his courage to reach for the brass knocker. Even before he touched it, the door creaked open.

"Come in," said a thin voice that was barely more than a whisper.

Soal entered the hut and came face to face with the witch. Within the deep lines of her face were the blackest eyes he had ever seen and the sight of her produced a lingering chill. Aware of her eyes never leaving his face, he pulled his gaze away to look around the hut. It was just the one room, dusty and strikingly bare, with just a few plants and herbs scattered around and a fire burning in the corner. The only item of any value was an elaborately decorated hand-held mirror lying on the table. It looked distinctly out of place within such a setting. The glass inside the frame reminded the prince of the witch's eyes, for it was so black that it seemed to hold no reflection.

"What can I do for you, Your Highness?" asked the old woman. There was no deference in her tone and the prince, so used to the feeling of superiority that was his birthright, felt uncharacteristically nervous. Although he wouldn't meet her eyes, he felt them burning into him.

"I've heard you have powers beyond this world," he said, "and I require your help and discretion."

The old woman continued to stare and the prince was suddenly aware that she hadn't once blinked. Despite the fire, he felt uncomfortably cold.

"Tell me, what is it that you desire?" she asked.

"My wife is a monster and I would be rid of her."

The words came out of Soal's mouth before he had considered them.

"Well," the witch replied. "Maybe we can come to some arrangement."

Soal suddenly had a feeling that his path had come to a crossroad. A voice deep within him screamed that he should walk out of the hut; that it wasn't too late. But before the prince had even heard what she was going to say, he knew that he wanted it.

His wife had brought an unpleasant and unfamiliar feeling of powerlessness into his life; a powerlessness that, more than anything else in the world, he longed to conquer. So now that a solution presented itself, Soal didn't stop to think about what it might cost. The prince's heart, which had already proved to harden at every chance to show compassion, now beat with a definite ruthlessness.

"What arrangement do you speak of?" he asked.

"I know someone who can make your wife vanish. But he will want something in return."

The prince shrugged. "He can have whatever he wants. There is nothing I hold more dear than my desire for her to disappear."

"That's no good," said the witch. "You must trade something you value."

Soal remained indifferent, so the witch continued.

"I will give you a piece of knowledge to barter with. Your wife is expecting a child. Would that be a price too high?"

"I offer the child, and with joy. Anything borne of that woman is of no value to me."

As soon as he uttered these words, a feeling of danger, like a blanket of sin, wrapped itself around him.

"As you wish," said the witch. As if from nowhere, she procured a single candle that she lit, and a goblet containing a dark liquid. Then she picked up the mirror and started humming, a simple, mournful tune. As it repeated, the flames in the fireplace began to die. The prince's uneasiness grew as the room became colder and darker until only the whites of their eyes were picked up by the candlelight. The humming stopped and the witch whispered, softer than ever,

"My Lord, the Unseen. I beseech thee, grant us an audience."

As she spoke, the mirror darkened until even the whites of their eyes could no longer be seen. Soal felt a rush of fear.

"My Lord," the old woman repeated, and the prince noticed that the quiet assurance of her voice was faltering. "You know what he asks. Would it please you to grant a prince his greatest desire?"

The mirror's surface rippled like liquid silver and the image of a young girl appeared. She was thin and ragged. Blackness once again shrouded the glass but the child's expression of fear and bewilderment had burned itself into the prince's eyes.

The next voice that came out of the witch's mouth had no tone and yet chilled the prince to his very soul.

"She shall be mine, and the little one too. And him... for a while."

A rasping laugh followed and the darkness slowly lifted once more into the dull shadows of the cottage.

"Well, my Lord." The witch's voice had resumed its normal tone, though she looked visibly shaken. "You have your wish and there's no going back now. All that's left to do is drink."

She picked up the goblet and Soal, with a feeling of dread, put it to his lips.

Chapter Nine

Soal was nowhere to be found and as the days turned into weeks, and then again, weeks into months, Helene became increasingly worried. It was not only she who was ignorant of his whereabouts, she sensed concern from others in the castle. For the first time, she dared to face his disapproval by sending messengers to seek out his whereabouts, but it was as if he had been swallowed into the ground.

One thing, however, had changed. Helene was with child. The months that went by were filled with hope and strength and she again endured her terrible nights without giving in to her baser instincts. As the witch had foretold, the princess gave birth to a baby girl who she named Kiana.

On the Wednesday that the child was born, eighty two guns were fired and trumpets sounded throughout the kingdom. Messengers were sent to spread the news all over the land. But to Helene's shame, the tender love she expected to have for her daughter never came. Kiana was born crying and seemed to never stop. Every night, Helene would cradle her daughter in her arms and sing to her, but still the baby wouldn't settle. And still the princess felt nothing. As Helene played and sang from morning until night, so would Kiana wail.

Doctors were brought in to attend to the infant but they could find nothing wrong. And as the days went by, Helene felt her detachment towards her daughter increase. Soal was still the only thing that occupied her thoughts. Kiana had brought hope, but the hope was impure: the princess wished that news of the child would make her husband return to her.

Shortly before Kiana's christening, an old woman appeared at the castle gates, requesting an audience with the princess. Although she was dirty and ragged in appearance, she claimed to have news of the prince.

Helene entered the room in a state of excitement and came face to face with the witch. Within the deep lines of her face were the blackest eyes she had ever seen, and the sight of her produced a lingering chill.

"What do you wish to show me?"

"It has come to my attention that your husband is missing and you long to find him. I can help you."

"Where is he?"

The witch presented an ornate mirror, and Helene saw herself, eyes wide with anticipation. Then the image in the glass shifted, and there was Soal. He was sat, rocking slightly, arms around his legs. It was very dark, but Helene could make out that he was in what looked like an enormous cave. His eyes showed no sign that they had ever smiled. The witch began to hum softly and he looked wildly around, as if he could hear the sound.

"Helene," the old woman cried, but it was the prince's voice that came out of her mouth. "I'm waiting for you."

Then the witch laughed, and the vision was once more replaced by her own reflection.

Helene's eyes filled with tears.

"I thought he didn't love me," she murmured, "but he does. It's his darkest hour and he's thinking of me. He needs me."

She turned to the witch.

"I must go to him."

"Your husband is trapped in the kingdom of the Unseen and it is a forsaken place. But if you are sure, I can help you reach him."

A fierce glint appeared in the princess' eyes as she responded,

"I don't care where he is. I will bring him home."

She dressed herself in a thick cloak and collected the one thing she could think of that might be of any use in a magical place – her enchanted harp. She strapped it tightly to her body and as if from nowhere, the witch procured a goblet containing a dark liquid.

Helene, with a feeling of dread, put it to her lips.

When the servants finally entered, there was nothing there but a few cherry blossoms and the cries of the princess Kiana, alone and abandoned by her mother.

Chapter Ten

elene found herself beside a black lake. The darkness surrounding her was thick and there was no sign of the opposite shore, but she had the feeling that the destination lay somewhere beyond her vision.

"Hello!" she cried, but her voice disappeared into the still air with no response. She waited a while, she didn't know how long, until the dark and the stillness started to play tricks on her mind, making her acutely aware of the air around her, which was heavy and painful to breathe. Then she remembered the tune the witch had hummed. It was like a magic key – as soon as the melody sounded from her mouth, she heard a rustle on the water and a boat appeared out of the gloom, its single swinging lantern revealing a cloaked figure. Helene stepped on board and without a sound, the boatman guided the boat back into the darkness.

The only thing to see was the lantern, swinging gently, but the dark around it seemed to close in on it to the point that it barely revealed its own form and certainly nothing more. Helene fleetingly wondered what its purpose was, as it served no use here. As Soal had discovered before her, in the absence of light and sound, time lost its effect to the point that a single second could have really been an hour and an hour a second.

At first this sensation caused her mind to alternate between a sedate floating feeling and wild panic but after a while she began to adjust to it and her thoughts settled into a muted rhythm, as though all joy and sorrow were tucked away.

After what felt like an age, and yet not, the boat slowed down and Helene felt it grind onto shore. Here she discovered what the use of the lantern was. As they had reached a series of large caverns that, although comprising of staggeringly large proportions, it was able to redirect the light enough to provide a ghostly impression of the space. The boatman moved towards the light and a skeletal finger, different to that of any creature she had ever seen, motioned for her to step out of the boat. As soon as she had set foot on land, the boat glided out again, leaving her back in the suffocating darkness.

"I don't suppose there's a light to be found anywhere," she mused. "Anyway, what good are eyes in the land of the dark? If light returns in this place, then so will sound. If I

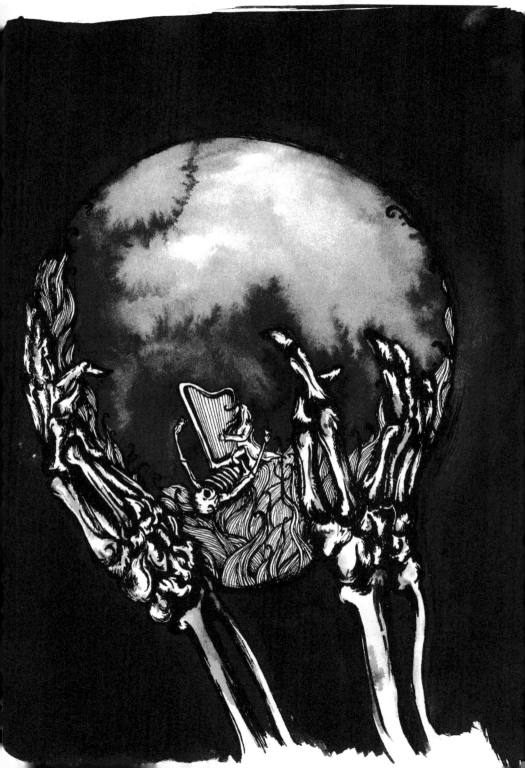

can't seek my prince, I may well bid him come to me."

And so Helene removed the enchanted harp from around her body and began to play.

Chapter Eleven

If it is true that love is selfless, well then, so, equally, is hate. In his bid to destroy his wife, the prince had never once considered what he himself might endure; yet the ill-conceived horrors that awaited him in the darkness of the Underworld did not distress him. On the contrary, he bore them with patience and even took morbid pleasure in these trials, reflecting always that Helene would soon be the one suffering them. However his months spent in this prison wore away at him until you may be sure that the vision Helene had seen in the scrying glass was no act.

The kingdom of the Unseen was as unbearable as you could imagine being locked inside a damp dungeon might be. Here there was no sun or moon, no difference of light, nothing, in fact, to signify the passing of time; and if it wasn't for the beating of his heart, Soal would have forgotten what a second felt like. There was also something wrong with the air – no breath, no matter how deep, seemed to satisfy. The prince realised he was breathing air that was not meant for his lungs. In this place, there was no single second of respite to be found.

Moreover, there was one final thing that made it clear to the prince that he was in no ordinary hell. Whenever his unwilling eyes grew heavy, the cold silence of the caves came to life. From the roofs of the caverns shone a harsh, flickering light, which made his head ache and all but blinded him. A low, intermittent drone filled his ears, inspiring an indefinable fear. The walls of the caverns were all made up of mirrors, and in those mirrors were many visions of himself doing indescribable things. In each reflection he had a terrible smile on his face and the reflection locked eyes with his own, acting out hellish deeds with a sickening slowness. Soal tried to close his eyes, but they were already closed.

Once, driven almost to madness, he ran all the way to the edge of the lake and dived in, but under the water the darkest impressions of his soul danced around him, touching his skin. He woke up in horror to find himself in the lake. The strange water surrounding him was already beginning to rot his flesh.

When awake, it was almost like the nightmares had never happened. But their residual dark hue over the prince's thoughts gradually deepened; eating away at Soal's sense of self.

After nine months in the kingdom of the Unseen, the man Helene came to rescue was very different to the one who had so resolutely sought out the torment that befell him.

Chapter Twelve

hen a person is pushed to the very extreme of what they can endure, it is safe to suppose that they change. Often it changes people for the better – it makes them stronger, kinder, and better equipped for the trials that lie ahead. It may not come as a surprise that this was not the case for Soal. The one thing that festered in him as strongly as ever was his hate for Helene and his will to destroy her. But he was a weak and pitiful specimen. There was no need of food or drink in the kingdom of the Unseen but instead his exterior was fed by his state of mind. Soal had lost an alarming amount of weight and, as Helene had seen in the dark glass, his face was sallow and joyless. One could surmise from a single glance that the time underground had starved his noble qualities and suckled the foul ones.

For the first time since he had drunk the witch's potion, Soal heard a noise. It was the harp. It's hard to imagine what an emotion this brought to him after so many months of silence. At first he was simply numb to the noise, as if it was coming from a forgotten dream, until it slowly caressed his ears and brought - alien to this place - a feeling of pleasure. Against his will, the princess' face surfaced in his mind and with it came a strange longing. A memory came to him from all those years ago, of those dark eyes gazing into him as though he were the only thing in the world that mattered. It was the same look, he thought, as had been in her eyes the last time he saw her. Those intimate moments - it struck him with a new understanding - that had meant so little to him but so much to her. It was almost enough to make one pity her. But he was past that; now a prisoner of the hatred that he had nurtured for so long. He had played over this moment - how he would look her in the eye and laugh as he told her that she was a monster who belonged in this place. And he was determined that no change of heart would steal from him what he had suffered so much to bring about.

Chapter Thirteen

elene's fingers swept over the strings of her harp, becoming more and more frenzied as the time passed and still no-one came. She played until her fingers bled. Still there was nothing to be heard, only the flat sound her instrument made in the indifferent caverns. But then, just as she thought she could play no more, she felt a hand cross the instrument, silencing the strings. She squinted through the thick air and her heart soared. It was Soal - his face was so close to hers that with the smallest movement of her chin she could have kissed him. But as she gradually made out his expression in the darkness, her joy evaporated. For in his eyes was a look of pure hate.

He grabbed her wrist forcefully, causing her breath to catch in her throat. Her eyes widened and she opened her mouth to say - what? Implore him to slow her thundering heartbeat?

"You monster," he hissed in contempt. "How long I've waited to give you the punishment you deserve."
His eyes bored into her with an intensity that melted the words on her tongue, and she began to shake.

"My love," she began, but he would let her get no further.

"I am not your love. I don't love you. And how could I? You are a creature of death and ruin."

Helene tried to stop the tears from falling down her cheeks. She had suffered so much to come this far and she wasn't going to give up yet. The years of misery had strengthened her, and so she continued.

"My love. The pain you feel hits me like a mirror. Wherever you go, you'll lead me; and if I am never to see the light again, still my only wish is to stay here in the dark with you."

"Why would you care if you never see the light again? You belong in the darkness. Don't you understand? I have led you here and therefore my pain has also been my pleasure. No more will you infect my thoughts and tarnish my days."

"Soal," the princess implored, her voice reduced to a whimper that felt ugly in her throat. "Please. You need to understand."

But as she spoke, the strength of her love began to feel like a weakness.

"I understand enough," he replied coldly.

"But I love you," she insisted. "I never told you how much I love you. The thought of you consumes my every breath and I see your shadow whenever I open my eyes. When I talk in my head, it's you I address. I have given my soul for your love and I would do it again a thousand times over. Why do you hate me so?"

The look Soal gave her made her feel like she was crumbling into the ground.

"Look at you," the prince said in disgust. "You're pathetic. You, the demon you are, begging for love? No-one will ever love you. You came into my world demanding everything from me. But I tell you again. Now that I have brought you here, you will never, ever, be set free."

The devastation that enveloped Helene's face would have broken a thousand hearts. But Soal's heart was as cold and hard as the ground he had lain on for so long. He was already finished with her.

Helene made her last attempt.

"We have a child. A little girl."

During his time in the Underworld, Soal had all but forgotten the witch's prophecy but these words brought back to him the sinister memory from the little hut. The blanket of sin that had felt so cold as it brushed over him in that place was now wrapped tightly around him, covering and comforting.

"Why would I rejoice in the child of a monster?" He laughed scornfully. "I am done with you and have nothing more to say."

And just as abruptly as he had grabbed her wrist, he let go. Before Helene could say another word, Soal whistled the witch's tune. The prince felt an unworldly pain, as though his body was being dragged through the stone itself, and then, just as he had been transported into his hellish prison, he was again released into the outside world.

Soal found himself back in the familiar hut and after so long in the darkness, even the somber gloom surrounding him burned his eyes. A few embers were glowing in the fireplace. But when he looked around, there was nothing to be seen but a few cherry blossoms lying on the ground.

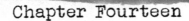

Chapter Fourteen

he whistle was the last thing Helene would hear for a long time. She was still reeling from her discourse with Soal; yet she couldn't accept the idea that her husband would have just left her here. So she waited for what must have been hours, straining her ears for the slightest noise. Then she again picked up her harp and played, and when she could play no more, she groped her way through the cavernous rooms, not knowing where she was or how long she had walked. At long last, the princess lay down and surrendered herself to sleep.

Unlike Soal, Helene had a resilience to the mirrored nightmares that presented themselves; perhaps because she was already so intimate with the darkest side of her soul. Horrifying visions of exposed bone and flowing blood were forced upon her but she experienced less of a haunting malice than the prince had been prey to. Yet alongside it was something different; seemingly a sign of something real. She saw Kiana slashing violently at portraits of her face with a knife until simply a black gouge remained. Soal was holding the young girl up to reach the paintings and the two of them were laughing maniacally. And though she hadn't yet been able to believe it, the princess now woke with the fresh realisation that she had been betrayed, that she was not loved, and that she was alone and trapped down here in the darkness.

And so Helene's quest changed. She knew the search for Soal would be foolish and fruitless, and her purpose now must be to find her way out of this eternal tomb. Without knowing for sure which way she was headed, she began to walk in the vain hope that it was back towards the way she had come. She stumbled as fast and as far as she had the strength to go. Then, for the first time, she encountered some luck. Just as she thought she mightn't be able to go on, her feet touched water. She felt a burning sensation and jumped back, wondering at this fresh torment she had stumbled upon. But this could not be the end. If Soal had found his way out - she thought, in a flash of anger - then so could she. She thought of the tune that he had whistled before he vanished. So she whistled, and waited, and whistled, and waited - to no avail. No-one was going to come and save her.

Well then, she would just have to save herself. She unbound the enchanted harp from around her body. Although she had no idea when, or even if, she would be back, she placed it carefully ten steps away in the darkness towards the left of the shore.

"Thank you, my friend," she murmured, "but you can't help me here. Stay safe until I return for you."

And with that, she dived into the lake.

The water closed thick around her and burned at every inch of her body. Yet she swam. She did not know if she was going forwards or backwards or upwards or downwards. All she knew was a pressure around her that suffocated her and ripped at her skin.

"I am going to die," she thought. "I'm going to die, and I don't care."

Still she swam, and the unendurable seconds lengthened into a rhythm. If only she could have seen herself, what a pitiful sight she would have witnessed. Her hair was reduced to strands clinging miraculously onto her shredded scalp and her skin hung off the bone in ribbons. The water moved like acid through her pores and into her veins. Yet still she swam.

It appeared that Helene would swim until her bones had eroded. So the Unseen surmised as he watched on in amazement. This woman was formidable. He had never seen anything like it. And as he watched, something very strange happened. The Lord Unseen, God of the Underworld, king of all things dark and dreadful, fell in love with the princess.

Chapter Fifteen

elene opened her eyes and looked around. She was lying on a pile of soft mattresses, a goblet of wine beside her. Remarkably, she felt no pain. She touched her arm, feeling her skin soft and smooth, with no sign of any wound; and she could feel her hair again falling heavy on her back as she sat up. For all she knew she might have been back at the castle, but for the otherworldly richness of the surroundings. The princess had grown up knowing nothing but lavishness, but this was eclipsed by the palace she was now in. The fabric she sat on was like nothing she had ever felt before and its thread shimmered in the soft light; yet she could not say where the light came from as there were no candles to be seen.

A mirror stood before her and Helene approached it with a mixture of curiosity and trepidation. But what she saw pleased her greatly. Her skin looked as soft as it felt, as though it had been bathed in some elixir. Her beauty was flawless; her eyes full of life. The dark shadows and sallow cheeks were gone and she was treated to a rare sight as her reflection smiled back at her.

"Do you like what you see?"

Helene started as she heard the voice from behind her and she turned around to see a man gazing at her. He was inhumanly attractive, with a face as devoid of flaws as her

own. The only thing conspicuously strange about him were his eyes: they seemed to hold no colour, or rather flickered between colours and shapes too fast for any one to stay in the memory. The movement drew her in like gravity and it was impossible to look away. Helene was hypnotised.

"Yes, I like it very much," she said shyly.

"Good." The man's lips looked like they never smiled and yet they were full and inviting, leaving Helene with a strange desire to kiss him. She wanted to ask where she was, but felt something holding her back from speaking, as if she needed permission.

"You want to know where you are?" the handsome stranger asked.

She nodded.

"You are my guest and you are safe. I won't let anything bad happen to you."

His words swept over her like a net of protection, yet some part of her felt uneasy.

"You are very beautiful and very brave," he continued. (She felt every word tingle all over her skin with a feverish pleasure.) "And I am in love with you."

At these words, the princess felt her heart swell with emotion, blocking her breath. Her single evening of true happiness with Soal had been tainted by the revelation of her curse. But now she recognised the dizzying feeling as it hit her for the second time in her life.

Please, let me linger forever in this moment, she thought to herself. But even as she entertained this plea, she felt darker thoughts being pushed away to the back of her mind. When she finally spoke, it was like breaking to the surface from deep water.

"Who are you?" she asked.

"I am the king of these lands. Some refer to me as the Unseen. But to you, I hope I may simply be Enesin, the one who you will never be parted from."

"I am in love with a god," thought Helene, and she felt exhilarated.

"You have drunk the wine of life and shed your human skin. I would have you as my queen. Will you say yes?"

"Yes," breathed Helene, and her only hesitation was through barely managing to speak.

And yet, even in this moment, while she felt like she might float away on a cloud of elation, there was something strange about the way this stranger made her feel, as if the wonderful spell she was under was just that, and beneath it there was… nothing. But the princess banished that thought from her mind as she melted into the ecstasy of falling in love.

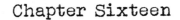

Chapter Sixteen

nd so, Enesin and Helene were married and throughout the whole time they were together, not a word was said about her union with Soal or their child. The other subject that was never broached was how the prince had come to be in the land of the Unseen in the first place. At first the new queen felt submissive and overcome by the king of the dead. She savoured each word of admiration he uttered; turning it round in her mouth again and again to prolong the effect. But it didn't take long before his power over her subsided. The initial thrill that had been inspired by the declaration of love from such a man faded faster than the queen had dared to imagine. It was superficial and meaningless and very soon it no longer brought any pleasure, or, in fact, any feeling at all. Although her life in Circan had been so marred by sadness, she found herself pining for it.

Unsurprisingly, she rarely thought of her daughter at all and the only thing that occupied her thoughts was Soal. In truth, not a single minute passed where she didn't think about him. Helene longed to rid herself of her love for the prince, but the more she tried, the more he consumed her every thought. She told herself what a pitiful and loathsome creature he was; how Enesin was his superior in every way. But the more time she spent with Enesin, the more she began to view herself voyeuristically, as though every tender moment with her new lover was nothing more than a show that the prince was somehow witness to.

As the months passed, these feelings grew into a simple desire to hurt Soal, but no matter how much she fantasised that she might rip his heart in two as he had done hers, she knew that she had no power over him. And so she began to fixate on her daughter as an accessory for revenge. Time went by as she entertained this plan, and the longer she spent turning it over in her head, the colder she became, and the more patient she grew. She would be most effective in biding her time. And so years passed as the new queen of the Underworld basked in the luxury her new life offered, and her cruel intentions did not subside over time.

Finally one day she decided it was time to appeal to her husband.

"My Lord," said Helene. "Back where I came from, I had a little girl. I am very content in my life here but I do think of her often."

She paused there, lest Enesin should muse on how far her longing might stretch. But the Lord of Death was, as one might suppose, a cold creature. He loved Helene but only as one might love a doll. He loved her because she was magnificent but his feelings didn't stretch to the need for requital. That was the blessing and the curse of the Underworld. Nothing could be felt with any depth, and empathy was a forgotten ability. It was something to do with the wine itself, that had washed all poignant emotion from their skin. Lines of laughter and sadness were eroded, leaving a dazzling but icy beauty. Beings outside of oneself were observed with a cool disregard. Enesin was aware of the motive behind Helene's request. But her feelings did not interest him.

"Of course," he replied coolly. "She must be brought here."

Helene, having prepared a case for her entreaty, was taken aback by the ease of the interaction. The king's reply was almost sinister in its simplicity and she felt like she was missing a piece of knowledge somewhere.

But true tragedy was about to strike; that which would make Helene's previous misfortunes appear as blessings in comparison. As her lust for vengeance might suggest, the queen's strong and pure spirit, heretofore indomitable through misery or pain, was eroding every day that she drank the wine of the Underworld. And as the beauty of her exterior increased, so too did the ugliness within.

Chapter Seventeen

eanwhile, back at the palace, Soal resumed his life. However he was visibly changed. He looked like an old man - his skin was creased and loose like soft yellow leather, and what hair he still had was wispy and sparse. The most dreadful change was in his eyes. They were haunted and hollow, without even a trace of the warm and infectious smile he had once held.

The courtiers were accustomed to the prince's frequent and unexplained absences. However prior to his reappearance, gossip over the departure of his quiet wife had travelled freely. Soal's return alongside his startling transformation fuelled this speculation until there was not an eye in the town that didn't regard him with mistrust. He spoke to no-one and no-one dared question him, but it could hardly be a coincidence that he had returned immediately after the princess had vanished.

The prince kept to himself, with no interest in anyone or anything. Years passed and still barely any change was effected. He hardly ate and on the rare occasion that the sounds of pacing stopped and he slept, chilling sobs could be heard from his chambers.

Sobs could also be heard from Helene's chambers where Kiana now slept. The little princess was a sickly creature. She was thin and pale and would break into tears at the slightest thing. Much of her time was spent in bed, out of the sunlight. The most learned doctors in the land were called but no-one could figure out what was wrong with her. And so she grew up like a ghost in the castle, fragile as a crystal of snow; and sorrow was her only companion.

Then, reluctantly, her father began to visit her bedside. Initially he felt nothing but coldness towards the child as he fought this unwelcome link to his wife. He would have stayed away but to dissuade his reputation among the courtiers for being cold-blooded. He knew that they watched him closely to judge among themselves whether or not he had the heart of a murderer. But gradually he began to visit of his own accord and his visits became more and more frequent. And as time passed, the tearful little girl inspired a long-forgotten tenderness in the prince's feelings.

Soal's love continued to grow; his face became less and less corpse-like, and he began to smile again. He spoiled his daughter with gifts and lavished affection on her. Occasionally, when the first evening star could be seen in the sky, he would manage to coax her outside. While he was with her, his memory of the Underworld all but disappeared. He spared very little thought and certainly no remorse for his cruel and arduous betrayal of his wife. But Soal was a fool to think that the magic he had set in motion was now behind him, and inevitably, the witch came to pay him another visit.

It was an evening in early Summer and the prince was out walking with Kiana among the blossom trees when he noticed the last tree on the left that he had ordered, as if in another life, to be chopped down. Soal was vaguely certain that it hadn't been there the day before but now it was as tall as it had ever been and in full bloom. As he tried to summon a hazy recollection, he watched a blossom fall. But before it hit the ground, as if out of nowhere, an old woman appeared before him. A dreadful feeling hit him as if he had been struck. Kiana felt it too and began to cry. But before the prince could react, the woman bent down and stroked the girl's cheek.

"Cherry wine?" she said, and, as if from nowhere, procured a goblet containing a dark liquid.

The prince began to shake uncontrollably and the deep hollowness in his eyes, which had been muted of late, returned. He thrust the little girl behind him.

"What do you want?" he said.

"Why, what you promised," said the witch, and her soothing tone with its gravel roughness was all too familiar.

The memory of his journey to the witch's hut felt like a lifetime ago but now a cold wave of dread began to seep through the prince's heart. The woman gave a scraping laugh.

"Have you forgotten already?"

With a bony finger, she beckoned to the child. "Hello, my pretty. Are you ready to go on an adventure?"

The horror inside the prince was building and for the second time in his life, all the authority he commanded was gone.

"No!" He fell onto his knees. "Please, I beg you."

The witch pulled out a dark mirror and even before it was turned, the prince knew what it would show. Nevertheless the moment played itself out: his own face appeared and there was a cruel glint in its eyes as his shadow self spoke.

I offer the child, and with joy."

"Please," cried Soal, holding the little princess tight. "I didn't know."

"The deed is done," declared the witch. "You promised the child and there's no going back now."

Soal grabbed Kiana's hand and turned to run but a sudden gust of wind knocked him off his feet. The sky above was black and drops of rain were falling faster and faster until they merged into one continuous flow. Through the curtains of water, the prince watched helplessly as the witch placed her arm around the child.

She lowered the goblet to Kiana's mouth.

"Drink this, my dear."

The young princess looked fearfully at her father, tears falling down her cheeks, and the sight was so pitiful that for a moment even the witch seemed to hesitate before she pressed the cup against the child's lips.

"Open up," she cooed, and she hummed that familiar melody.

Kiana vanished and Soal, reduced to all fours, was violently sick in the grass. When he looked up again, the sky was clear and there was nothing to be seen but a few cherry blossoms scattered on the ground.

Chapter Eighteen

iana's disappearance could not be ignored by those inside the palace, already so suspicious of the absence of the prince's gentle wife.

Soal stayed in his room for three days, admitting no one and not leaving his bed, but on the third day the door was forced open and soldiers came in to arrest him. They presented him with a warrant that read:

Sentence for the Prince Soal Aquilana, pronounced against him by this court, to be put to death by the severing of his head from his body for crimes of the unlawful killing of his good wife and his daughter, aged seven. The said sentence will be carried out in the open street before Angelo Cathedral upon the morrow being the thirtieth day of this month of July between the hours of ten in the morning and five in the afternoon of the same day with full effect. And for so doing, this shall be the warrant. All officers and soldiers and other good people of Circan are required to witness this act.

The prison he was thrown into was oddly comforting - darkness and stone around him was such a familiar feeling and made him aware, with gratitude, of the air that didn't hurt his lungs. And as he lay on the ground, he knew how he needed to spend his final moments.

As the prince instructed, the soldiers searched for a hut deep in the forest with an old woman inside. The witch, with her mirror, was escorted to the dungeon and as the prince's final wish, he was left alone with her.

The door was closed and Soal was once more face-to-face with the woman's empty black eyes.

"What do you desire?" The words came out of her mouth as a hiss.

"I need your help," he said. "I need to reach someone"

"You can see the girl," she responded, "But you won't reach her. However, if that is what you want..."

"Not her," the prince replied, and the witch stopped in surprise. "There is nothing that I desire more than to speak to my wife."

The witch froze. "You surprise me," she said impassively, but the prince was aware that what little colour her face had held was suddenly gone. "Surely you don't want to torment your final thoughts."

"I desire only this."

The witch showed no expression, but the hand that now held the mirror up was shaking ever so slightly.

She whistled her tune and the gloom of the dungeon around them grew black. And then from the mirror, Helene's face appeared. Her face, contrary to the gentle eyes that he knew, held a terrible beauty, and her expression was as hard as ice. She stared at him.

"What could you possibly have to say to me?"

It might have been accompanied by a laugh of triumph if the queen was not so completely humourless.

"Tomorrow I will be put to death," Soal said, "but first you need to know, our daughter has joined you in the lower world."

And at that moment, as he said those words, he realised the monstrous sin of his betrayal.

"Of course I know," the queen replied coldly. "I brought her here."

"No, you don't understand," whispered the prince. "It was me. I made a deal. I sold her and I sold you, and with it I sold my soul. I am sorry. With all my heart, I am sorry. I am a broken man and I regret the wrong I have done to you."

Helene's distant fantasy had finally presented itself - *he* was there in her mirror, face to face with her. How long she had waited for this moment; how the idea had consumed her every thought. How she had imagined savouring every word; turning it round in her mouth again and again to prolong the effect. But now as the words were delivered to her, she felt... nothing.

Then the image in the glass faded and the vision was once more replaced by her own dazzling reflection and the beautiful room surrounding her. But something new had stolen into her passionless expression - a glint of discontent.

Chapter Nineteen

he next day Soal met his final fate through a public beheading in the town square.

But as Helene's revenge was complete, she knew it was no revenge at all.

Chapter Twenty

here is my daughter?" Helene asked some days later, after nothing had been said on the subject.

"Everything has been taken care of," Enesin responded.

"So when will I see her?"

"I'm sorry," replied the king impassively, "but that is out of the question."

Helene was in shock. "I don't understand," she said.

"There's nothing to understand. Are you not happy here, with me?"

Helene nodded. "Yes, of course I am. But why can't I see her?"

The king's eyes momentarily flashed with a muted anger that immediately subsided as if it had never been there, but the glimpse of this filled Helene with fear.

"You will do well not to worry yourself about her," he said, and there was a hint of tonelessness in his charming and resonant voice.

Although the conversation was closed, the feeling of discontent that Soal's appearance had inspired was growing, and it was beginning to break through the hard shell of the queen's soul. And as this feeling grew, with it grew a strange longing for her daughter. Helene had been shaken out of her subdued comfort, and consequently she finally began to reject the world around her. The prince's words echoed in her head and began to haunt her. *No, you don't understand. I made a deal.* Something was very wrong and she determined to find out what it was. One day she placed a sponge beneath her clothing and when the king turned away, she poured the wine she was given down her chest, to be soaked up in secret.

For seven days Helene repeated this action, and each day, the world around her gradually began to dissolve. To her indescribable horror, the beauty that had adorned her surroundings began to morph back into the desolate caverns that, up until now, had been but a distant memory. The magnificent table she sat at for dinner was nothing but damp ground and the bedroom, with all its finery, was simply a corner of the cave. Helene's husband, the handsome King Enesin, was becoming less handsome every day, until at the end of the seven days not only was he revealed as the most repulsive creature the princess had ever laid eyes on, but a stench similar to rotting flesh emanated from him. When she looked into his eyes, all that could be seen was a single endless black hole.

Sharing his bed was now the most unendurable thing Helene had ever experienced, but she bore it, knowing that secrecy was her key to survival. She was resolved to discover the truth, and only then would she truly have nothing to lose. Helene began to wander farther and farther away from the cave she had been living in. Although the wine no longer altered her senses, the world around her was different still to her first experience. Previously in the caverns of the Underworld she had seen nothing but thick black air closing around her. But her body had adjusted over her years in the kingdom of the dead. The air still felt heavy in her lungs but she was now able to see through it, although there was not much to see but vast caves and an empty horizon.

One day Helene began walking and didn't stop. She walked for what might have been

hours or even days. After miles and miles of nothingness, she was rewarded by something familiar - she stumbled onto the lake where it had all begun. She was now able to see the water seething and frothing with the poison that had so horribly mutilated her body. On the shore was a gnarled, rotting tree, covered in the first signs of life Helene had seen here. Worms and maggots were crawling out of its many cavities and as the queen looked closer, she saw that its roots reached down to the lake. They reminded her of veins and she shuddered as she thought of them drinking that water. As her gaze travelled up the branches, she saw rotten clumps that on closer inspection must be flowers, with virulent looking berries amongst them. It evoked a distant memory - another tree from another world.

As the queen reflected on this, an instinct told her to hide - of course there was nothing along the shores of this forsaken place to conceal her, but she backed as far as she could go until she was pressed against a wall, and from there she saw something nearing the tree. Although far away, the sight of its scuttling movements caused her to shudder. The creature laid down a sinewy basket and began to clamber up the trunk, jumping on the branches and striking them so that the fruit would fall. Yet it was only as it clawed its way down and began to gather the rotten berries into the basket that Helene realised with true horror the source of the wine that had so veiled her senses.

Chapter Twenty-One

elene dared not return to Enesin - she had walked too far and for too long. Now that the king's spell was lifted, there was only one thing on her mind. She must rescue her daughter.
She thought back to that distant day where she had plunged into the lake to defy her fate. Retracing her steps along the shore, she was amazed to discover that her enchanted harp was right where she had left it. Helene strapped the harp to her back and turned back towards where she had come from. She walked with purpose but every cave looked the same and it wasn't long before she had lost all sense of direction. The queen was now more afraid than she had ever been in her life. She didn't know what Enesin would do when he found her but her mind kept replaying the toneless voice and dark flash of his eyes. Helene knew without a shadow of a doubt that the King of the Underworld did not forgive. Now that the wine's poisonous charm was lifted from her, the world around Helene was a dark and ugly place, and if she had seen her own reflection now she might have cried, for the immense damage that the toxic water had done to her body was again visible. However just as her physical beauty had inversely affected the state of her soul, so it was that she now felt cleaner inside, and we can be sure which reality our beautiful and brave heroine would rather choose.

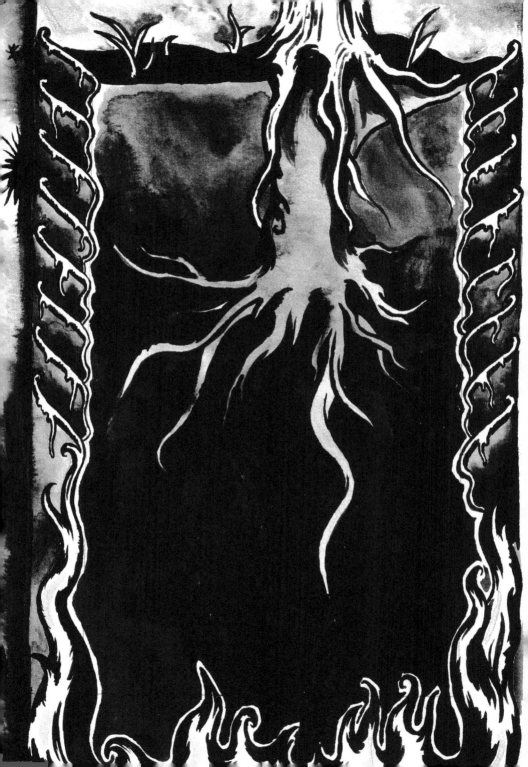

Finally, overcome with pain and fatigue, Helene sat on the floor and began to weep. The tears poured down her face with no sign of stopping and began to collect in a crevice on the floor. Helene wept and wept as if her heart was breaking, and the tears continued to fall until they had formed a pool on the ground of the cave. Suddenly, a melody from the distant past came into her mind. It was the witch's tune. In the midst of her sobs, she hummed it. The dark pool of tears at her feet came to life, bubbling and shimmering, and the cave was so silent that from the ripple of the water, words could be deciphered.

"Gentle queen, what troubles you so?"

The distraught queen drooped in sorrow, no longer questioning this strange but familiar magic.

"I have lost everything," she sobbed. "As a result of my terrible cruelty, my own daughter is somewhere in this forsaken place. I know she suffers horribly."

The pool seethed and frothed at the edges while the princess continued to weep as if she might never stop.

"If you have any heart, you will help me," she entreated through her tears.

The festering pool was now rising in waves, and the crash of their impact echoed violently through the silence of the cave.

"My dear. Go back to your husband and forget about the child."

But at these words, Helene now raised her face from the ground. The tears in her eyes were now replaced by a fury that flashed dangerously. She lifted her chin and her heart pounded with rage.

"Oh, you evil spirit," she cried. "Never again will you come to me when I am weak. Never again will you offer the path of sin as if it were the path of salvation. And never again will I heed your wicked words."

As Helene spoke, the waves stopped and the colour of the water began to change. The pool of tears was changing from a festering blackness to a clear calm that glistened like silver in the gloom. Then it began to disappear as if it were being sucked into the thirsty ground. As this happened, the queen heard, as if from deep underground, a muffled scream so terrible that it stopped the blood in her veins. And then the crevice was once more as dry as if water had never touched it.

Helene's anger had awoken a feeling of power. Upon witnessing this new magic, the princess felt overcome with bravery. She thought back to every change in her life that she had effected. Her first flight from the window. Her journey to seek her husband. Her swim through the lake. And now her quest to find her daughter. She had nothing to fear and nothing to lose.

"I was a slave to the night," she cried, and the cave resounded her words loyally ("night, night, night") "But now I am its queen."

Then she took out the harp and began to play. She played for the first time since Soal's betrayal, and this time it was not to summon, nor to conjure, but simply for the joy of playing. She played as if she had never stopped, and as the notes sounded, the world around her faded. Nothing was real except for the tremor of the golden strings as her fingers glided over them.

utting through her trance, Helene suddenly became aware of the sound of light, hesitant footsteps. Through the murky gloom a figure could be seen; a ragged, skeletal child with a shadow of a face that seemed to hold no feature except for large, dark, scared-looking eyes. At first the queen was speechless, then she cried out with joy and opened her arms. But at this, the little girl drew back.

"Please," Helene implored, "don't be afraid. I am your mother."

The little girl looked yet more terrified and then began to run. Helene hurriedly strapped the harp to her body as the sound of the child's feet faded farther and farther into the distance. She hastened after her daughter, straining her ears to hear the faint footsteps. Then the sound came to a sudden halt. Helene felt a cold chill move through her body and it took all her courage to keep walking. The feeling of power she had embraced was rapidly fading as she caught the familiar smell of rotting flesh, and she struggled against the paralytic fear of what she was about to face.

Out of the darkness appeared Enesin in all his dreadful majesty. He was touching Kiana's neck with one hand and the child's mouth was open in a silent scream.

"Just where did you think you were going to go?"

It might have been accompanied by a laugh of triumph if the king was not so completely humourless.

"You belong to me. The girl belongs to me. The deal was made and can not be undone."

At the sight of her daughter in the hands of the King of the Dead, the fear dispersed

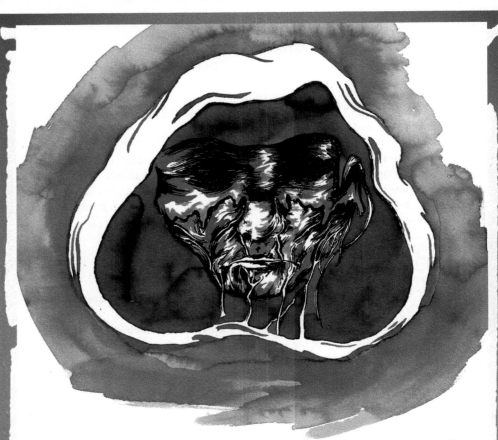

and Helene began to shake with rage.

"You are wrong," she cried furiously. "Neither my daughter nor I belong to anyone."

"But you do. Don't you see how completely I own you? You are bound to me. You were given to me. And you consented to be mine. For better or for worse."

Despair began to engulf the queen. But suddenly, as she looked at her child in the hands of this devil, a wonderful thing happened. The gaping hole that Soal had left in her heart was filling up with love for her daughter. She could feel the maternal instincts that previously had so evaded her. After all the loss and betrayal and cruelty, something beautiful was blooming inside her. The feeling brought her back suddenly to her childhood and she remembered something. From the very deepest recesses of her mind surfaced long-forgotten words that she knew instinctively to contain great power. She grabbed the girl's hand and looked the king deep in the gaping darkness of his face while she whispered:

"Pearl to pebble, silk to hay
Night winds bear your joy away"

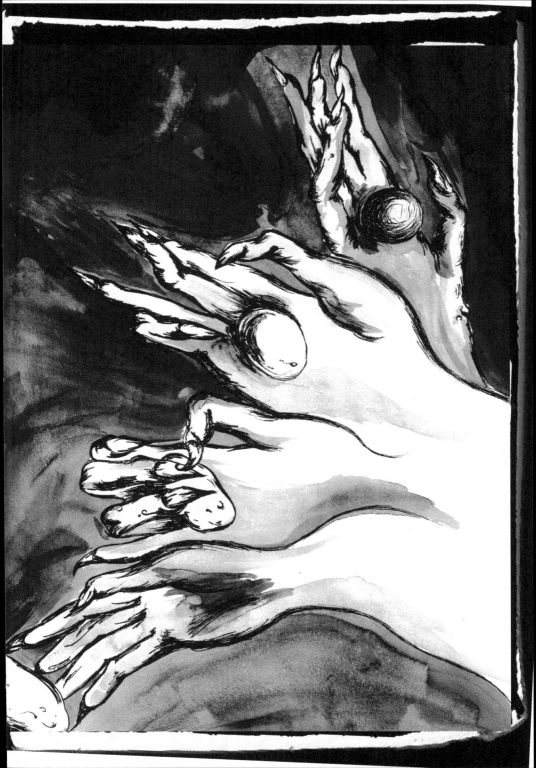

Chapter Twenty-Two

s soon as she spoke these words, she felt the old familiar pain as her bones began to crack. But this time she welcomed it, for she knew that the change held a magic beyond Enesin's rule. Her wings opened into their full magnificence and before the king could react, Helene gripped Kiana's hand and flew. Together they shot back through the caverns and over the black lake. The forgotten moonlight of Circan burned her eyes as she flew them farther, into the forest beyond. Kiana had fainted from pure terror. The night air that swept around Helene was agonising - each breath of wind ripped at her skin and her areas of exposed bone ached dangerously. But her vision began to adjust and through her pain, she was awestruck by the beauty of the world around her. The stars above, scattered like seeds of light, sparkled as though another world - more brilliant still - was leaking slowly through the sky. The forest, though black green, stood out from the blanket of the night with a luminosity that defied the darkness. As they circled the forest, Helene spotted a small hut. Holding her daughter's unconscious body close, she hit the ground and dragged her talons clumsily towards its single rotting door.

She approached the brass knocker in trepidation, but before she could reach it, the door creaked open of its own accord. The hut was dusty and strikingly bare, with just a few plants and herbs scattered around and a fireplace in the corner. A mirror lay on the floor and Helene picked it up in surprise. It was the same mirror that the old woman had presented to her, all those years ago. The glass was deformed as though it had somehow melted off the frame. There was something sinister about it and the queen looked around the room uneasily. However there was nothing to be seen but what appeared to be a few shrivelled cherry blossoms scattered on the ground.

Helene shuffled slowly outside, her mangled legs buckling under the strain of her wings, and, gripping Kiana tight, took to the air again. In the distance a sunrise threatened and it gave the queen an overwhelming feeling that time was running out. Soon she reached a familiar sight. In the distance, the turrets of the castle could be seen, silhouetted against the looming sun. She had very little strength left, but as the wind attacked her broken body, threatening to tear through her flesh, the queen looked down at her daughter and the same determination that had carried her into the acid lake of the Underworld once again flooded through her. Ahead was the solitary tower where her chambers lay. The window was firmly shut but with all her force, Helene propelled herself into it and the two of them tumbled onto the familiar carpet amid a pile of broken glass.

The large mirror stood at the corner of the room, covered in its heavy drape, and the sight of it evoked ugly feelings of shame and sinfulness. Helene lay on the floor, her desecrated form resembling a pile of rags. Her body was no longer fit for this world.

As her breathing became shallower, the queen felt a heavy pain in her heart - the familiarity of the room around her brought with it all the memories of her sorrowful existence in the kingdom of Circan. Blood tears filled her eyes with the fresh weight of the isolation she had been so accustomed to, and she knew that she had never belonged in this place.

awn was imminent. With the last of her strength, the queen stretched out her arm and hooked a talon over the drape of the mirror. As she did so, Kiana stirred and slowly looked up. Helene, with her pale, bloodied eyes, turned to her, and the princess held her gaze. To the queen's astonishment, the young girl's face was filled not with horror, but with love.

"Mother," Kiana whispered.

At this sound, the queen's face contorted with pain and streams of red began to cascade down her cheeks. Overwhelming feelings of sorrow and happiness tugged her heart from either side and a bubble of emotion was rising inside her. It pushed at her lungs and filled her body until her jaw clenched open in a silent sob.

"My darling," she said. "I love you."

Kiana, sobbing also, threw herself around the fading queen's wings.

As the gentle weight of her daughter fell against her, the heavy drape fell from the mirror. From the corner of her eye, it seemed to Helene that the air was catching under it as though it were not velvet, but silk. She remembered her mother's words. *Promise to always keep it covered after nightfall.* She closed her eyes tight and pain convulsed through her.

The drape hit the ground just before the first sunbeam crept over the horizon and the last of the fading moonlight bounced from the mirror's face, returning to Helene. She squeezed her eyes shut as she felt it pierce the centre of her heart and spread through her like a wave. Kiana too felt its force and held her tighter.

"Mother, look," cried the little girl. "Look in the mirror."

Helene looked up and what she saw astonished her. Expecting to come face to face with the pale, filmy eyes that had so horrified the prince, she saw a very different vision. She was not soft and delicate, nor pale and seductive; neither did she exhibit the ethereal and doll-like beauty that had so fascinated her in the mirror of the Underworld.

But her dark eyes held a brightness that she had never seen before, and there was something radiant about her that filled up the room. Her body was no longer skeletal and ragged but strong and smooth, and, more extraordinary still, she was elevated from the floor. Then suddenly she knew. *This is what it looks like to be loved.* And all of a sudden she understood the advice her mother had given her for what it was; and realised that the queen had known no better but to live in fear and shroud herself in darkness.

Helene looked at her daughter. "I love you," she said again. And then suddenly, in a moment of profound clarity and forgiveness, "You've got your father's eyes, you know; eyes that always look like they're smiling. He loved you too, more than anything in the whole world. My darling, you have been so loved."

As she uttered these words, she felt a lightness in her heart, such as she had never felt before.

"Mother, you're beautiful," the girl cried.

For the first time Helene could see her true self: her beauty was reflected through the love in her daughter's eyes. She stood up and something extraordinary started to happen. Her body - the broken vessel that had for so long borne such pain and suffering - was changing. Just like the stars in the sky above, an otherworldly radiance was breaking from inside her. Light poured out of her skin, as if her soul was escaping from the prison of her body.

"You're leaving," Kiana whispered.

"Yes I am," said the queen sadly. "But let me leave you with these words. I know that your heart will always be good and open and true, and with this, you will know the only thing that matters: to love and be loved in return."

Kiana went to embrace her mother a final time but her arms closed onto emptiness. The air was filled with grey flakes, and dusky chalk covered the young princess. There was no ragged body; no monstrous wings; nothing, in fact, but a pile of ash. Kiana looked down, then up again, and then walked over and placed her hand on the mirror, hoping to catch a final glimpse of her mother. But Helene was gone and the orphaned princess was alone, her wishful hand meeting only its own reflection. The girl's eyes shone like dark moons from her face. She felt a deep sadness, but for the first time in her life, the tears never came. And on the air floated a haunting melody - her mother's final lullaby.

The words I say, soliloquy
My echo weighs like gravity
But all I ever needed to learn
Is just to love and be loved in return
That is the answer, my child, and now you know

Milton Keynes UK
Ingram Content Group UK Ltd.
UKHW022304200524
442847UK00005B/52